# Lizards for Lunch
## A ROADRUNNER'S TALE

WRITTEN BY Conrad J. Storad • ILLUSTRATED BY Beth Neely and Don Rantz

The RGU Group

Being Different Makes All The Difference™

*Tempe, Arizona*

The illustrations were rendered in watercolor and with pen and ink
The text type was set in Esprit Medium
The display type was set in Latiara
Composed in the United States of America
Art direction and design by Trina Stahl
Editing by Conrad J. Storad
Production supervision by Todd Atkins

Printed in China

First impression

Library of Congress Catalog Card Number: 98–65000
ISBN-10: 1–891795–00–7—Softcover
ISBN-13: 978-1-891795-00-8—Softcover

The RGU Group

www.theRGUgroup.com

16 15 14 13 12 11 10 9 8 7   (sc)

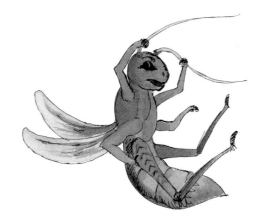

Hello! Glad to meet you
Listen close, hear my tale
I live in Southwestern deserts
With coyotes, jackrabbits, and quail.

Please call me Roadrunner
The fastest bird on the ground
Don't do much flying
I run in quick bursts that astound

I'm a strong and proud bird
Though great beauty I lack
I have odd, skinny feet
Two toes point forward, two back.

Snip, Snap, Crackle, Munch!
For breakfast I gobble up bugs by the bunch
Crickets are chewy, beetles go crunch
A hungry Roadrunner likes lizards for lunch.

Mom and Dad fed us lizards
Brought them right to our nest
They were plump, soft, and chewy
Fat ones with horns tasted best.

My long beak is sharp
My legs are quite strong
I like to run through the desert
I can run all day long.

Life in the desert is tough
There are dangers for me
I will fight if I must
But I run to stay free.

I spot my food from far off
Because my eyesight is keen
But running all day
Keeps my body quite lean.

Listen close in the desert
You might hear my loud call
Cooing notes to my family
*Coo coo-ah coo-ah coo-ah*

Snip, Snap, Crackle, Munch!
For breakfast I gobble up bugs by the bunch
Crickets are chewy, beetles go crunch
A hungry Roadrunner likes lizards for lunch.

My feathers are buff brown
With a green and bronze sheen
I have black and white speckles
Colorful bright eyes that gleam.

I run through the brush
Wings spread and flapping
The noise scares up insects
My mouth begins snapping.

Hoppers buzz this way and that
I snatch them with my long beak
The bugs are delicious
But it's fat lizards I seek.

Some lizards have black collars
Or colored stripes that all match
But one thing is certain
Lizards are real hard to catch.

Some lizards are wiggly
Some have horns and thick skin
To catch one is tricky
It takes quickness to win.

To fight a horned lizard
Can be quite a scene
Puffed like a big spiked balloon
The creature looks mean.

I'll eat mice, bugs, and spiders
Small snakes are a treat
But it's lizards I love
Their taste can't be beat!

Snip, Snap, Crackle, Munch!
For breakfast I gobble up bugs by the bunch
Crickets are chewy, beetles go crunch
A hungry Roadrunner likes lizards for lunch.

# Roadrunner *[Geococcyx californianus]*

| | |
|---|---|
| **Weight:** | 6 to 8 ounces |
| **Length:** | 20 to 25 inches, beak tip to tail tip |
| **Diet:** | Mice, insects, lizards, snakes, scorpions, spiders, small birds |
| **Color:** | Brown with green sheen, streaked with black and white |
| **Song:** | Series of low cooing notes: *Cooo cooo cooo-ah cooo-ah* |

THE ROADRUNNER is the world's fastest-running flying bird. It prefers running to flying. Roadrunners zoom along the ground taking as many as 12 steps per second. While being chased by a car, roadrunners have been clocked zipping across the desert at speeds up to 15 miles per hour. The speedy bird got its name long before the automobile was invented. Roadrunners ran on trails alongside cowboys on horseback or on roads next to ranch families riding in wagons and carriages.

The roadrunner can change direction very quickly as it runs. The bird uses its long tail like a rudder on a boat to help it turn. As it runs, the roadrunner leans forward and straightens and extends its long neck. It uses its tail and wings to stay balanced. The roadrunner's speed helps it to get away from predators such as coyotes and hawks. Quick moves make the roadrunner very good at catching flying insects, mice, snakes, and lizards. Roadrunners also have excellent eyesight. They can spot a lizard skittering towards rocks yards away while watching an enemy hawk circling overhead at the same time.

People have many other names for roadrunners. About the size of a skinny chicken, the roadrunner actually is a member of the cuckoo family. In Texas, the bird is called a chaparral cock. In New Mexico, people call roadrunners "the lizard eater" or "the snake eater." In Mexico, roadrunners are called the *paisano*. The name is from a French word that means "comrade" or "fellow countryman." The Mexican people consider roadrunners as "little friends," because the birds like to eat snakes.

When hiking through the desert, you might see a roadrunner with a long snake dangling from its beak, just like a long noodle. The roadrunner's stomach is not big enough to hold the entire snake. The bird swallows an inch or two, then rests. After part of the snake digests, the roadrunner eats another few inches. Then rests. Eats. Rests. Until the whole snake is gone.

Roadrunners live in the deserts of the southwestern United States and throughout Mexico. They make shallow, saucer-like nests near cactus or among scrubby desert shrubs and bushes. A female roadrunner usually lays three to five eggs once per year. After the chicks hatch, both mother and father roadrunner protect the nest. They also take turns bringing food to the babies. Hungry roadrunner chicks gobble down bugs, grasshoppers, crickets, mice, frogs, small snakes, and lizards of all kinds. Fat, horned lizards taste best!

Tim Trumble

**CONRAD J. STORAD** grew up in Barberton, Ohio, amidst the belching smokestacks of tire factories, steel mills, and auto assembly plants. He didn't see his first roadrunner, javelina, saguaro cactus, scorpion, or rattlesnake up close and personal until 1982, when he began graduate school at Arizona State University. Currently, Storad is the editor of the nationally award winning *ASU Research Magazine,* and is the founding editor of *Chain Reaction,* a science magazine for young readers. He also is the author of many science and nature books for children and young adults, including the titles: *Don't Ever Cross That Road!, Don't Call Me Pig!, Little Lords of the Desert, Tarantulas, Scorpions, Sonoran Desert A to Z, and Saguaro Cactus.* Storad lives in Tempe, Arizona with his wife Laurie and their miniature double dapple dachshund, Sophie. They enjoy hiking and exploring the wilds of the Sonoran Desert.

Steve Rolwing

**BETH NEELY AND DON RANTZ** met while studying fine art at Northern Arizona University in Flagstaff, Arizona. They soon discovered that they had a mutual attraction to the outdoors, gardening, cooking, reading, and each other. They married in 1993 and there began their artistic and lifelong collaboration.

Presently, they reside in a small historic bungalow in Prescott, Arizona with their two cats, and a backyard menagerie of birds, lizards, raccoons, skunks, coyotes, and even a small herd of javelinas. These surroundings provided them with the means from which to draw inspiration as the illustrators of the children's book *Don't Call Me Pig!,* which preceded their work in *Lizards for Lunch: A Roadrunner's Tale.*